W9-BSB-637

© 2004 Disney Enterprises, Inc.
All rights reserved.

Published by Scholastic Inc.
90 Old Sherman Turnpike, Danbury, Connecticut 06816.

No part of this publication may be reproduced in whole or in part,
or stored in a retrieval system, or transmitted in any form or by any means,
electronic, mechanical, photocopying, recording, or otherwise,
without written permission of the copyright holder.

SCHOLASTIC and associated designs are trademarks and/or registered trademarks
of Scholastic Inc.

For information regarding permission, write to:
Disney Licensed Publishing
114 Fifth Avenue, New York, New York 10011.

ISBN 0-7172-6816-0

Designed and produced by Bill SMITH STUDIO.

Printed in the U.S.A.
First printing, March 2004

The Missing Gift

A Story About *Trust*

by **S.R. Baecker**
illustrated by
S.I. International

SCHOLASTIC INC.

New York   Toronto   London   Auckland   Sydney
Mexico City   New Delhi   Hong Kong   Buenos Aires

The sun was directly overhead when
Pocahontas guided her canoe onto the riverbank.
Nakoma and her friend Dyani were waiting to
greet her.

"Hi. How did you know when I'd be back?"
Pocahontas asked.

"Your father told me," Nakoma explained.

"But where did you go?" Nakoma asked.

Pocahontas looked surprised. "Didn't my father tell you?" she asked.

"No," said Nakoma. "He acted as if you were on a secret mission."

"So what's the big secret your father wouldn't trust me with?" Nakoma whispered.

Pocahontas smiled. "Oh, it isn't really a secret," she said.

"My father asked me to pick up the special necklace he had one of the Weanocks make for Kekata the medicine man," she explained.

"So, let's see it!" Nakoma said excitedly.
Pocahontas grabbed her leather pouch and
tossed it gently to Nakoma.

But the pouch slipped through Nakoma's fingers and plopped into the river.

"Whoops, sorry," Nakoma said, kneeling down and grabbing the pouch out of the water.

$\mathcal{N}$akoma slipped the necklace out of the pouch. "It's very nice. Kekata will be honored to wear it," she said, handing the necklace to Dyani.

"It's beautiful!" Dyani exclaimed. "Can I try it on?"

"No, I'm sorry, Dyani," Pocahontas said.

"Why? I won't ruin it," Dyani protested.

"It's a gift. It wouldn't be right for someone else to wear it," Pocahontas explained.

"*F*orget the necklace, Dyani," Nakoma said. "Let's all go swimming."

"Good idea," said Pocahontas. "Please put the necklace in the pouch, Dyani, before you come in the water."

"I will," she said, admiring how it sparkled.

$\mathcal{T}$he girls swam and played in the water until
the sun had moved across the sky to the other side
of the river.

"It's getting late," Nakoma said.

"Yes, we'd better go," Pocahontas agreed.

*O*n their way back to the village, Pocahontas felt Meeko tugging at her pouch.

"Meeko, stop!" she said sternly. "There are no nuts or berries in it for you. There's just the neck— Oh no! The necklace isn't here!"

"Dyani, didn't you put the necklace in the pouch?" Pocahontas asked.

"No. I put it *on* the pouch!" Dyani said.

"It probably slid into the canoe," Pocahontas said, hoping she was right. "You and Nakoma go on ahead. I'll get the necklace and meet you later."

$\mathcal{P}$ocahontas looked everywhere, but she could not find the necklace.

"It must be here," she thought, "unless Dyani wasn't telling the truth. No one else has been here . . . She's the only one who could have it. Oh, I don't know what to think."

*P*ocahontas walked towards Nakoma's home. "Did you find the necklace?" Nakoma asked when Pocahontas returned.

"No," Pocahontas said. "Dyani, if you don't have it, where could it be?" she asked.

"*I* don't know. Maybe Meeko buried it or Nakoma took it," Dyani said angrily.

"I would never do that!" Nakoma said.

"And I would? You don't trust me, either," Dyani cried, running out of the house.

"I need to talk to her," Nakoma said.

"There's someone I need to talk to, also," Pocahont thought. "I'll see you later," she said.

*P*ocahontas left Nakoma's and headed for the glade to talk to Grandmother Willow.

"Grandmother Willow! Grandmother Willow!" Pocahontas called as soon as she saw the limbs of the magical and wise tree.

"What is it?" Grandmother Willow asked.

"I've lost a very important necklace. I know it's terrible of me, but I think Dyani, Nakoma's friend, took it," Pocahontas quickly explained.

"Oh, dear," Grandmother Willow said. "There can be no other explanation?"

"No. None," Pocahontas said. "Nakoma was there, too, but I know she would never do such a thing. I trust her completely."

"*B*ut Dyani you do not trust?" Grandmother Willow asked.

"I just don't know," Pocahontas replied.

"Then you must find out," Grandmother Willow urged. "And if you are wrong, apologize and show Dyani that you trust her. A necklace has been lost. Do not lose a new friend, as well."

"Thank you, Grandmother Willow," Pocahontas said.

"I'm glad you came to me, dear," said Grandmother Willow. "Just remember, things are not always as they appear." Then her face slowly disappeared into the bark of her trunk.

*P*ocahontas left the glade and searched the path back to the river. Nakoma was sitting on the canoe, obviously troubled.

"Nakoma, don't be upset. It's not your fault the necklace is missing," Pocahontas said.

"*I*'m not upset about the necklace," Nakoma said. "I can't find Dyani."

Just then Dyani came running towards them. "I've found it! I've found it!" she called.

"*I*t's up there," Dyani said, pointing.

"Where? I don't see it," Nakoma said.

"Just below the top of the cliff—hanging from that bird's nest," said Dyani.

"How did it get there?" Pocahontas asked.

"There's your answer," Dyani said, pointing to the sky.

A large raven was flying overhead. A string with shiny stones dangled from its claws! The bird flew to its nest, dropped the stone necklace, and flew away.

"Ravens are attracted to shiny objects," Dyani said. "It must have swooped down and grabbed your necklace while we were swimming."

"Let's get it back from that robbing raven!" Nakoma shouted.

"*I* can reach that," Pocahontas thought. Then she remembered Grandmother Willow's advice: "Show Dyani that you trust her."

What would a princess do?

"Can you reach it, Dyani?" Pocahontas asked.

"Let me try," Nakoma offered.

"Oh, no, you've already dropped it in the river once today!" Pocahontas said, teasing. "I think we should trust Dyani with the necklace rescue."

"You're right," Nakoma agreed.

So Dyani carefully bent over the edge of the cliff and grabbed the necklace.

"Thank you, Dyani," Pocahontas said, sliding the necklace into the pouch. "And I'm sorry for the way I behaved today."

"I'm sorry for the way I behaved, too," Dyani said.

"So, are the three of us all friends again?" Nakoma asked.

Pocahontas and Dyani smiled at Nakoma. "Yes!" they said together.

"And if we ever doubt each other again," Pocahontas added, "we should remember this day."

The End